SOCIAL DISTANCE

OR

SOCIAL DISTANCING...

Are words that mean a lot of things.

Social distancing might mean some time away from school...

We can play, but learning is still cool!

You'll probably spend more time at home...

But that does not mean
you are alone!

Mom or Dad may be home too...

But that doesn't mean they
don't have work to do.

You will be with your family...

And can play fun games, like Monopoly!

So what are some things to be done?

Reading books is always fun!

Or you might have a movie night...

The one with Jedis you might like!

Did you know that while you wash your hands...

You can sing songs from your favorite bands?

Social distance, may mean playing less with friends...

Stay close with a call or letter,
until you see them again.

There's grandma, grandpa and others who....

Would be happy to hear from you!

When you get hungry,
can you please...

Help to cook some Mac 'n' Cheese?

Ask your dog and they may

BARK...

For a walk in the yard and
not the park.

What else shall we do? Well let's see...

How about a tea

PARTY!

Excuse me,
but I would
like to ask ....
?

Why do some people wear those face masks?

Remember, listen to parents and loved ones...

Because being safe is smart

and **FUN!**

Now that you have learned so much about social distancing....

I declare you the Social Distance King or Social Distance Queen!

Dedication

's book is dedicated to all the people in our country and throughout the world that · selflessly working to care for the sick. Of course, it is also written for the children, ·d-working parents and adults working together through these trying times. I would o like to dedicate this book to my father, family and friends. I wrote this book while :ial distancing. During this time, I was reminded that when you're "close" to neone...even when you're not close...you're close. No distance can keep love from ing with you. I hope this book can be helpful as together we heal and overcome.

Author Books

Be sure to check out other fun and spirited children's books by author Eric DeSio available at www.BeYouBooks.com

Friend Ships™ Series

Be You™ Series

The Social Distance King™

Catch 22™

#ImToo™

CPSIA information can be obtained
at www.ICGtesting.com
Printed in the USA
BVHW010621020920
587370BV00003BA/4